BETWEEN PANIC AND DESIRE

Between Panic and Desire

by Bear Kosik

Published by: bearly designed
www.bearlydesigned.com

Cover photography by Bear Kosik

ISBN-13: 978-0-9976570-4-3

bearly designed

Between Panic and Desire

by

Bear Kosik

CHARACTERS

MARK:	Male, mid-thirties.
CARIDAD:	Female, late thirties.
ESPERANZA:	Female, late twenties.
DR. GREENE:	Male, early thirties.

SETTING

The sitting room of an older house in Indiana, Pennsylvania.

TIME

February 2 of the present year.

SCENE ONE

Setting: A comfortable sitting room with a sofa, chair, coffee table, side table, and lamp. Hooks for coats are along a wall beside the front door of the house. Winter light streams in from windows at the sides and unseen windows downstage. A dining chair facing upstage sits at the edge of darkness behind the sofa. A deck of cards, pencil, notepad, and can of mixed nuts are on the coffee table. A landline telephone is on the side table.

At rise: MARK is speaking to someone on the telephone. He alternately stands and sits restively, although getting up is difficult due to a bad knee. He uses a cane while standing and walking around.

MARK
(sharply, but not loudly)
I said I would hold. … What do you think I've been doing for the last ten fucking minutes and most of the last forty fucking minutes?
(CARIDAD enters from the rear.)
I'm sure you don't want me to use expletives, but I find them perfectly valid when speaking to incompetent people giving me the run around.
(softly, to CARIDAD)
Do you need the phone?

CARIDAD
No.

MARK
It's not a question of me calming down. I already told you. I am calling because you cut off my disability benefits by mistake and my disabilities include psychological trauma triggered by people who have jobs and treat me like shit, because I am unemployable and I don't treat people like shit unless I am shat upon.
(to CARIDAD)
It is 'shat', right?

CARIDAD
(shrugging)
How would I know?

                    MARK
Why can't you just call me back when you have an answer
instead of wasting my time staying on hold?
                    (voice rising, barely under control)
Really? … You could have done that forty fucking minutes
ago and didn't tell me? … Goddammit! Why the hell didn't
you tell me? … Oh, for Christ's sake! … Fine, but I expect
to hear back by noon or I'm gonna rip some office jockey a
new orifice.

          (MARK ends the call.)

                    CARIDAD
          (sitting on the sofa)
Mark, why are you getting so worked up over losing your
benefits?

                    MARK
          (still agitated)
Why shouldn't I?

                    CARIDAD
You just inherited over a million dollars.

                    MARK
Money I don't want or deserve.

                    CARIDAD
Why? Because your father was estranged from you?

                    MARK
          (calming down)
We weren't estranged. He just never thought about
contacting me after he started drinking again.

                    CARIDAD
He never came back to see you or Momma even while he was
sober. That's estranged in my book.

                    MARK
          (becoming annoyed)
Yes, Cari. You're right. How can I forget my father was
kicked out of here when I was eight and never once came
back to see his only child?

                         CARIDAD
                    (trying to be empathetic)
          My father did the same thing, you know.

                           MARK
          But your father never married Momma.

                         CARIDAD
          Breeding bastards is no excuse for being an absent parent.

                           MARK
                    (calming down again)
          You're right. Neither one of us had caring fathers.

                         CARIDAD
          At least your father cared enough to leave everything to
          you.

                           MARK
          Dying intestate is not an act of love.

                    (MARK sits in the chair and grabs the pencil
                    and notepad from the table to write down what
                    he just said.)

                         CARIDAD
          Hoarding another gem for future use?

                           MARK
          If I don't, I'll forget.

                         CARIDAD
          Are all writers sponges like that, soaking up proverbs and
          platitudes wherever and whenever they find them?

                           MARK
          You'll have to ask all writers to get an answer. Or at
          least enough until one says 'No'. This writer does. They
          make great writing prompts when I get stuck.
                    (After setting down the pad and pencil, MARK
                    leans back in the chair, looking far more
                    relaxed.)
          Anyway, getting Dad's money isn't an intentional act on his
          part. Like all good alcoholics and addicts, he just
          procrastinated and never got around to drawing up a will.

                         CARIDAD
Does that mean bad alcoholics and addicts are better at
looking after their affairs?

                          MARK
Yes, smartass, as a matter of fact they are.

                         CARIDAD
I see. Which category are you?

                          MARK
I always went above and beyond to make sure no one could
complain about my drinking and drugging.

                         CARIDAD
Didn't anyone find out?

                          MARK
If they did, they never confronted me about it. In the
Army, they only care that you follow orders and get the job
done.

                         CARIDAD
I remember Momma calling me when you went into rehab. She
was in shock her decorated veteran son needed treatment.

                          MARK
I wish she had shown as much surprise when I came back from
my second tour with my mental problems.

                         CARIDAD
Come on! She was always concerned her children were going
to have psychological issues.

                          MARK
I don't know why.

                         CARIDAD
I always assumed it had something to do with our fathers.

                          MARK
The only thing I know is that we've never been allowed to
talk about them.

                         CARIDAD
Aunt Shirley and Aunt Janet have said some things…

                         MARK
Really?

                        CARIDAD
Do you ever tell anyone that Aunt Shirley's boys may be
your half-brothers?

                         MARK
And make it sound as though we come from some backwoods
holler? No way. Besides, the court established they were
your dad's kids.

                        CARIDAD
Only because Dad didn't contest the paternity suit. To be
honest, I think he'd take credit for every baby born in
town if he could. I lost count how many half-siblings I
have.

                         MARK
I never have been comfortable with the half-sister thing.
Makes it sound like you're half a person.

                        CARIDAD
That's very sweet of you.

                         MARK
I *have* wanted to pretend Ranza isn't related at all, ever
since her father went nuts.

                        CARIDAD
Which leads us back to your rant with the person on the
phone.

                         MARK
I can't help it. When I'm triggered, I lose control.

                        CARIDAD
I get that. What I still don't understand is why you're so
concerned about your benefit checks being stopped when you
know you will be getting so much money from your father.

                         MARK
Money I won't see for another year according to the letter
I got. In the meantime, what am I supposed to do?

                        CARIDAD
We can sort something out. It's only temporary.

                           MARK
No. It's one of those things. I was contributing to my
upkeep through that benefit check. Now, I have nothing.

                         CARIDAD
You have a mortgage free house and two sisters who don't
mind helping you out.

                           MARK
I'll be dependent on you.

                         CARIDAD
Why is that a problem?

                           MARK
I just said. It's one of those things.

                         CARIDAD
You could ask the executor about giving you an early
distribution of some of your inheritance.

                           MARK
That'll make it seem like I'm greedily waiting for the
estate to be settled.

                         CARIDAD
No, it will show that you have a justifiable, immediate
need.

                           MARK
A need I wouldn't have except for some idiot's mistake in
stopping my benefits.
                    (becoming agitated again)
I shouldn't have to be in this position. I shouldn't have
to take charity from you. I shouldn't have to ask the
executor for an early disbursement.

                         CARIDAD
                (exhausted and caring)
Shouldn't, shouldn't, shouldn't. Yes. You shouldn't have to
do anything. In fact, you don't have to do anything. But
that still leaves you with the same need to be filled.

                           MARK
Which should be filled by them continuing my benefits. I
have a valid reason for getting them. I earned them after
having my knee shattered and my psyche scrambled.

                    CARIDAD
And now you have an equally valid reason for asking the
executor.

                     MARK
Except, it's not. It's based on someone's mistake that
should be corrected.

                    CARIDAD
So, let Ranza and me cover your expenses while you fix this
mistake.

                     MARK
               (calming down again)
You've got moving expenses and you're already picking up
the difference on Momma's rent. Besides, Ranza's not of
sound mind to agree.

                    CARIDAD
No one has determined that Ranza is no longer competent.

                     MARK
Deliberately wrapping your car around a tree just to have
that experience doesn't strike me or anyone I know as the
act of a sane person.

                    CARIDAD
Anyone you know? Who have you talked with?

                                        BLACKOUT

Between Panic and Desire

SCENE TWO

> (MARK is downstage looking out as though through a window. CARIDAD is sitting on the sofa playing solitaire.)

MARK
I thought you were going to pick up Ranza.

CARIDAD
I am in a little while.

MARK
I'm glad you're moving back home from Texas. I won't have to rely on Mother if I can't drive. He was a saint taking care of me when I had my wisdom teeth removed when Momma was away.

CARIDAD
How is the old Mother Hen?

MARK
He's fine. He still advises the LGBT student group at IUP even though he retired.

CARIDAD
That group was one of the best things about going there for college.

MARK
(moving away from the 'window')
Yep. I'll never forget when I walked in as a freshman all set to meet other gay guys. Instead I found my older sister.

CARIDAD
That was classic. Of course, Mother forewarned me that he had received an email from a Mark Hogsdon asking about the location of the meeting. I had to laugh you were using Momma's maiden name. If you had used your real surname, he never would have known I was your sister.

MARK
And you said nothing and just waited for me to show up.

                    CARIDAD
Are you kidding? I'd do anything to get around having to
come out to you, or anyone for that matter, by saying 'Look
at me! I'm a lesbian!'

                    MARK
           (standing behind CARIDAD)
You know, that's some of the best advice anyone ever gave
me. Just be myself and let other people figure out which
bus I'm riding. I found out in the Army that the guys who
could care less about my sexual orientation knew pretty
quickly.

                    CARIDAD
And the ones who were prejudiced?

                    MARK
Nothing. They were too ignorant to put two and two together
to make three.
           (pointing to the cards)
Speaking of which, two of hearts under the three of clubs.

                    CARIDAD
What about the people in your group therapy?

                    MARK
           (idling around with his cane)
We have enough issues going on that being narrow minded
about anything isn't healthy.

                    CARIDAD
I still can't believe you went to a bunch of vets with
PTSD, addictions, and other assorted disorders to discuss
your sister's sanity.

                    MARK
Are you kidding? Go with the experts, right?

                    CARIDAD
That's nuts.

                    MARK
Oh, that reminds me. We're almost out of mixed nuts.

                    CARIDAD
In this house?

                    MARK
               (smirking)
Yeah, hard to believe. And that's another thing. Without my
benefit check I can't afford the pistachio blend.

                    CARIDAD
Is 'pistachio blend' crazy code for something?

                    MARK
No, smartass. It's a special kind of mixed nuts that Ranza
bought for me.

                    CARIDAD
Aside from containing pistachios, what makes it so special?

                    MARK
It doesn't have Brazil nuts.
               (eagerly)
Did you know Brazil is named for Brazil nuts?

                    CARIDAD
How do you know the nuts weren't named for the country?

                    MARK
Because the nuts were named first.

                    CARIDAD
How do you know?

                    MARK
Because I was there!

                    CARIDAD
No, you weren't.

                    MARK
               (sitting down in the chair)
I certainly was. Right after the first chicken hatched from
the first chicken egg, someone said 'we ought to call these
here black-shelled, claw-like nuts Brazil nuts.'

                    CARIDAD
Immediately after?

                    MARK
No, first we oohed and aahed over the chick.

Between Panic and Desire

                    CARIDAD
                 (sarcastically)
How cute!

                    MARK
Anyway, Brazil nuts are in deluxe mixed nuts, which is much
better than regular mixed nuts. Regular mixed nuts is …
are? … is half peanuts.

                    CARIDAD
A lot of people like peanuts.

                    MARK
That's not the point. Peanuts don't deserve to be mingled
with nuts. They are legumes like beans and peas.

                    CARIDAD
          (sitting back from the card game)
Okay, I remember now. It's another one of those things. Did
you ever hear back from the Planters people asking them to
stop calling peanuts nuts?

                    MARK
Yep. They sent me a lousy two-dollar off coupon for the
purchase of three of their products.

                    CARIDAD
That doesn't sound so lousy if their pistachio blend is
pricey.

          (CARIDAD goes back to the card game.)

                    MARK
Okay. Two dollars is kinda generous.

                    CARIDAD
Remember how Ranza's father would go to the bank and get
two-dollar bills to give as tips in restaurants?

                    MARK
I still have some.

                    CARIDAD
I do to, somewhere.

                    MARK
I bet that's what happens to a lot of two-dollar bills.

                         CARIDAD
True. You never see them in circulation.

                         MARK
Unless you have a crazy stepfather doling them out just to
make a point.

                         CARIDAD
What was the point?

                         MARK
To make people aware they exist, I guess.
               (MARK picks up the can of nuts on the table)
You know that coupon put me over the two-thousand-dollar
mark in apology stuff I received last year.

                         CARIDAD
Two thousand? That's a lot of coupons.

                         MARK
It wasn't just coupons. The total included a free oil
change, a fresh turkey, and some bigger items.

                         CARIDAD
Bigger than a turkey?

                         MARK
Bigger in terms of value, smartass.

                         CARIDAD
I'm surprised anyone responds to your rantings. Doesn't
paying off a complaining customer only encourage more
complaints?

                         MARK
I'm sure someone at Wharton or whatever did a study and
discovered it's worthwhile to be beneficent to those of us
who carp to the point complaints are escalated.

                         CARIDAD
It sounds like bribery to me.

                         MARK
There's no quid pro quo. They're just handing me a lollipop
to keep me quiet. I'm not agreeing to hold back on
criticizing them.

                    (CARIDAD ends the card game and places the
                    cards exactly where she found them.)

                              CARIDAD
Except you do, don't you? Once you're bought off with a
coupon or gift card, you stop complaining.

                               MARK
About that particular incident, sure. But it's not going to
stop me from complaining later on if they don't fix the
issue or a different issue arises.

                              CARIDAD
                    (standing)
And they never wonder if you're just scamming them?

                               MARK
I always offer ways for them to change what they do so that
no one has to complain in the future. They've taken my
advice a couple of times.

                              CARIDAD
I'd go nuts if I complained about every little error
companies make.

                               MARK
That's why it helps to be a nut already.

                              CARIDAD
I thought you were a legume.

                    (MARK cautiously moves to the sofa.)

                               MARK
That would be you, the family lez-bean.

                              CARIDAD
                    (ignoring the remark)
Anyway, I meant the futility of complaining. You're trying
to change the world one error at a time.

                               MARK
I would much rather have a better customer service
experience and not have to complain than to get all those
gift cards, credits, and coupons.

                    CARIDAD
And here I thought you were just chasing after a Nobel
Peace Prize.

                    MARK
I gave up on that dream a long time ago. It went with all
the others.

                    CARIDAD
'Went with all the others.' Don't start with the poor me's.
I have to pick up groceries. Then I'll pick up Esperanza.
Dr. Greene told her he would stop by once she's home.

          (MARK stretches out on the sofa.)

                    MARK
Who's Dr. Greene?

                    CARIDAD
The new psychiatrist on staff at Regional, apparently. I'm
surprised someone like him would choose to live in the
wilderness of Indiana County PA.

                    MARK
A-ha! So, he's good looking.

                    CARIDAD
How would I know? I haven't met him yet.

                    MARK
Then what did you mean by 'someone like him'?

                    CARIDAD
A young professional who I gather is unmarried. Hey, did
you watch the show from Punxy this morning. Did Phil see
his shadow?

                    MARK
I recorded it. We can watch together once Ranza is home.

                    CARIDAD
Sounds good.

                    MARK
Until then, spring will be in a quantum state of being six
weeks away and not at the same time.

                    (MARK grabs the notebook and pencil.)

                              CARIDAD
Saving that one for posterity, too?

                               MARK
Yep.

                              CARIDAD
Okay. See you in a couple hours.

                    (The telephone rings as CARIDAD exits upstage
                    into the darkness. MARK answers the telephone.)

                               MARK
Hello? … Yep, this is Mark Forrester. … December twenty-
seventh, nineteen eighty-three. … Six-zero-seven-eight. …
What happened? … Are you serious? … Why would you let her
do that? … Yes, she's my mother, but I'm not a child. … For
Christ's sake, I revoked the power of attorney. … Do you
realize where she is? … Why would you allow her to do that
without checking with me? … Great. … Look, I was already
furious that you stopped the benefits. Now I am beyond
furious. I need to speak to a supervisor right now. … Yep,
I'll hold.

                                              BLACKOUT

SCENE THREE

>(MARK is sprawled on the sofa napping. He mutters. He punches a pillow, then kicks. His body shudders. He wakes up with a start. He doesn't immediately sit up. He cautiously turns his head to evaluate where he is. As he sits up, he continues to look around to orient himself. He leans back into the sofa and looks up, mouth open.)

MARK

Damn!

>(ESPERANZA enters from upstage.)

ESPERANZA

Hello, Big Brother. I'm home.

>(ESPERANZA stands behind MARK. She looks down into his face.)

MARK

Damn!

ESPERANZA

Uh-oh. Did you just wake up from one of those dreams, Big Brother?

MARK

No. I'm trying to catch snowflakes.

ESPERANZA

Silly! It doesn't snow indoors. At least, not since the roof was patched where the meteor hit the house. Do you remember that, Big Brother? That rock from space tore a big hole in our roof even though the rock wasn't all that big. The fire chief thought the meteor exploded on impact.

>(ESPERANZA begins to wander around the room looking at things aimlessly and checking now and again to see if MARK is paying attention.

MARK remains on the sofa, face looking up, eyes
open.)

                        ESPERANZA
We looked all over trying to find fragments in the yard.
Never found a thing. Do you remember? The homeowner's
insurance said a meteor was an Act of God and they weren't
responsible for anything God did. When the preacher heard
that he told Momma the congregation would accept
responsibility for God throwing a rock at our house. Then
folks at the church had a bake sale and donated money to
help us pay for the new roof. Of course, the preacher
couldn't explain why God would throw a rock at our house
and damage the roof in the middle of winter. That's when
Momma stopped going to church. She was grateful for the
assistance the congregation provided us in our time of
need. But Momma didn't see much point in worshiping a God
who put a hole in our roof in the middle of winter.
            (ESPERANZA peers down into MARK's face.)
Of course, she would have been pissed off with a God who
did that in the summer, too, I think.
            (ESPERANZA looks up trying to see what MARK
            sees.)
Anyway, Momma stopped going to church. You must have been
twelve. We were never baptized on account of that meteor,
you know.
            (ESPERANZA leans down and kisses MARK on the
            forehead.)
Stopping going to church was the sanest thing Momma ever
did other than throwing my Daddy out. Do you remember, Big
Brother?

            (MARK slowly lowers his head, swivels on the
            sofa, and looks up at his sister.)

                          MARK
What the hell are you talking about? Are you still drugged
up from the hospital?

                        ESPERANZA
Well, yeah, probably. But that's no way to welcome me home.

                          MARK
How am I supposed to welcome you when you walk in, loom
over me when I'm still half asleep, and start rambling on
about rocks and God and Momma and roofs?

                    ESPERANZA
          (sitting down)
Roofs! That's funny the way you say it. Say it again.

                    MARK
No.

          (MARK stands with difficulty using his cane.)

                    ESPERANZA
Come on. Just for me! Say 'roofs'!

                    MARK
I said, no.

                    ESPERANZA
Meanie!

          (MARK walks downstage to the 'window' and looks
          out.)

                    MARK
Stop it! Besides, what are you doing here? Where's Caridad?

                    ESPERANZA
Cari dropped me off. And what do you mean, what am I doing
here? I'm living here. Doctor Greene said I'm not allowed
to live by myself for a while. I need supervision.

                    MARK
And who's going to supervise you here?

                    ESPERANZA
You and Caridad, silly.

          (MARK turns and walks back to the sofa.)

                    MARK
You're joking! I'm not fit to supervise a goldfish. And I
don't know any Doctor Greene. He never asked me if I wanted
to supervise you.

                    ESPERANZA
Why would he have to ask? You're supposed to look after me.
That's what Big Brothers do.

          (MARK sits on the sofa.)

                    MARK
Then I've been doing a lousy job of it. What brother lets
his sister do what you did?

                  ESPERANZA
             (almost leaping from the chair)
Lets?! Lets?! Come on! I acted intentionally and willfully
for good reason.

                    MARK
Good reason? Really?

                  ESPERANZA
Good enough for me. I certainly didn't need your permission
or Cari's or even Momma's to make a decision like that.

                    MARK
Then what do you suppose is the rationale for placing you
under my and Caridad's supervision?

                  ESPERANZA
That's my point. I was in no need of supervision until
after I landed with my car splashed against a tree. Seconds
before that anyone would have said I was perfectly sane and
required no supervision whatsoever. Out popped the air bag.
Bang! I must be crazy. Now someone has to watch me, as
though I'm going to do something like that twice. Such
nonsense. Who's silly enough to believe that? Especially
once that air bag bashed me. Do you know those things hurt?
My worst injury was a bruised jaw thanks to that sack of
gas. It felt like a satin fish smacked against my face.

                    MARK
             (reaching for the pad and pencil)
Can I use that satin fish line sometime?

             (ESPERANZA stands and walks behind the sofa.)

                  ESPERANZA
Sure, sweetie. Anything I say cannot be used against me in
a court of law, but it can wind up in anything you write
with my blessing since everyone will believe it is pure
fiction.

                              MARK
Speaking of fiction, Dear Sister, they didn't keep you in
the hospital for eleven days of observation for a bruised
jaw.

                            ESPERANZA
Of course not!
                    (She leans down into his face.)
Everyone thought I was bat-shit crazy for driving off the
road and hitting a tree because I wanted to have that
experience.

                    (ESPERANZA straightens up and walks to the
                    'window'.)

                              MARK
Are you saying that's not crazy?

                            ESPERANZA
Not for a second.

                              MARK
And for denying that, you were hospitalized, sanitized, and
rationalized.

                            ESPERANZA
I was certainly not rationalized. I gave them one good
reason I did what I did.

                              MARK
Which was?

                            ESPERANZA
I told them it wasn't any different than if I paid someone
to take me up in an airplane so I could jump out believing
a little sack of silk like that air bag was going to save
me from slamming into the ground, like the parachuting you
did in the Army.

                              MARK
That was your defense for what you did?

                            ESPERANZA
Didn't I just say so?

                              MARK
And they said 'okay, she's not crazy' based on that?

                    ESPERANZA
They had to. The logic is perfect. If I had gone skydiving
instead of driving, no one would think nothing of it.

                      MARK
Anything.

                    ESPERANZA
              (turning to face MARK)
What?

                      MARK
No one would think anything of it.

                    ESPERANZA
Oh. I just said nothing that way to make me sound innocent
and vulnerable.

                      MARK
Is that how you talked your way out of the hospital?

                    ESPERANZA
            (sitting in the chair again)
I didn't need to talk my way out of the hospital. I gave
them the one good reason they asked for. I used logic to
counter their arguments. I behaved every day. I followed
all protocols and procedures. And, most importantly, I told
them I was not going to make a habit out of wrecking
vehicles while driving them.

                      MARK
Leaving the door open for you to wreck parked vehicles? Or
should I say *more* parked vehicles?

                    ESPERANZA
How do you know about that?

                                            BLACKOUT

SCENE FOUR

> (ESPERANZA is using the
> landline telephone. MARK is
> pacing with the use of his
> cane.)

ESPERANZA

Yes, I'll hold. … After deliberately running my car off the road, I have nothing better to do than sit here listening to music someone thinks is relaxing.

MARK

Why'd you tell them that?

ESPERANZA

I didn't. You know the drill. They put you on hold before you can respond to them asking if you mind being put on hold.

MARK

Then why continue talking? People are going to think you're crazy.

ESPERANZA

People in this house?

MARK

Not *us* people.
> (pointing out the 'window')
Those people.

ESPERANZA

> (leaning forward and squinting to look where
> MARK is pointing)
What do I care about those people? They aren't real.

MARK

How can you be sure?

ESPERANZA

Nothing outside my ken is real. If I can't see it, smell it, smack it, or suck it, it isn't there, doesn't exist. And never trust anything you hear. You never know if those are actual people talking or voice- Hello? Hello?
> (ESPERANZA hangs up.)

                    ESPERANZA (cont.)
They did it again. How is it possible to lose a call every
time you transfer it to a coworker?

                    (ESPERANZA stands as MARK sits down on the
                    sofa. She paces around the room.)

                    MARK
Incompetence. Apparently, the only people allowed to have
steady jobs any longer are those who don't know what the
hell they're doing.

                    ESPERANZA
Oh, not that again, Big Brother. We all know how
frustrating it has been for you. I warned you that butting
heads with your superiors was going to lead to disaster.
There's no use holding onto that resentment.

                    MARK
Easy for you, Dear Sister. You aren't saddled with being
unemployable thanks to standing up to no good managers
trying to twist the last drops of blood from turnips. Every
single time I encounter someone who is doing a lousy job
just reopens the wound and inflames all the tissue.

                    ESPERANZA
That doesn't mean you have to tell them what they are doing
wrong or how to do a better job.

                    MARK
Why not? Someone has to tell them or they're going to
continue to do a bad job.

                    ESPERANZA
Isn't that up to their supervisors?

                    MARK
Who I usually wind up speaking with.

                    ESPERANZA
You just have to get past that anger.

                    MARK
How am I supposed to get past it when it's thrown in my
face almost every day that people who can't do their jobs
go home with paychecks and I can't even get a gig cleaning
toilets?

                              ESPERANZA
Certainly not by dwelling on it, Big Brother. It's been
three years. Time to let go.

                               MARK
Let go of what, the wheel like you did?

                              ESPERANZA
Why not?

                               MARK
You're one hour out of the monkey house and already trying
to convert others to your holy cause of flipping out and
giving in to the voices. Explain again how the hell they
decided to release you.

                              ESPERANZA
Well for starters, I didn't tell them voices told me to do
it, that's for sure. I didn't tell them I planned on
leading a crusade against sanity as soon as I was free
either.

                               MARK
I've got to give you credit for that.

                              ESPERANZA
                 (sitting on the arm of the chair)
I don't deserve credit for using common sense. After you've
been 302'd, you have to get it switched from involuntary to
voluntary admission ASAP, right? You do that by admitting
you acted just a little bit psychotic, because if you admit
you're insane they know you aren't. You participate in all
group stuff and cooperate with all directives. But when
someone opens the door and says 'go frolic' you do not leap
and tumble into the wide world. It may only be a test. No,
you solemnly step into the sunlight, breathe deeply, and
graciously bid the jailor adieu. Only after he has closed
the door and you hear the keys jangling as he walks away do
you jump for joy and somersault as rapidly as possible to
the nearest refuge for those who are no longer deemed
insane enough to keep imprisoned. Usually, that refuge is
your family home.

                               MARK
That refuge is the incubator for your insanity.

ESPERANZA

True. It's familiar and therefore easier for us to relax,
loosen the restraints of convention a bit, and maybe even
howl at the new moon on a pitch dark night. But this place
isn't the reason we go bonkers. It could be the place we
find serenity and contentment. It's just a matter of-
(The telephone rings. ESPERANZA jumps to answer
it.)
Yes, this is she. … Thank you, but I'd be happier if the
connection didn't drop than to receive your apology. … Yes,
I need my prescriptions. … Sure.

MARK

Hold again?

ESPERANZA

Uh-huh.

MARK

Bastards. Calling you back because of their mistake and
then they put you on hold. Whatever happened to courtesy?

ESPERANZA

Video games.

MARK

What?

ESPERANZA

You know. Pow-pow! Blam-blam! Blow up her! Cut him in half!
All those video games Momma never allowed us to play have
destroyed civilization. Everyone is too focused on what
they need, what they are doing. People don't know how to
react to others, and they don't have consequences if how
they act is poorly received.

MARK

That's a lot of baggage to place on one cultural
phenomenon.

ESPERANZA

One cultural phenomenon that has been thoroughly pervasive.
Think again, Big Bro—Oh! Yes! I'm still here. … What? … No.
… Fine.
(She hangs up the phone.)
All that and the only thing they can say is 'wait until you
see Dr. Greene'.

(ESPERANZA begins pacing again.)

MARK

When is that?

ESPERANZA
(reading from the palm of her hand)
My next appointment is February fifth at ten o'clock a.m.

MARK

Can you last three days?

ESPERANZA

I guess I'll have to.

MARK

You'd think those people at Regional would know enough to give patients their medications or the scripts for them when they're discharged.

ESPERANZA

Now that I think about it, they didn't even know who was picking me up or what time.

MARK

Cari was supposed to make the arrangements late yesterday. Idiots!
(suddenly remembering)
Hey, you never said where Caridad headed off to.

ESPERANZA

She wanted to get the grocery shopping done.

MARK

She said she was going to do that before she picked you up.

ESPERANZA

I guess she didn't.

MARK

Why would she say she was going to the grocery store before picking you up and not go to the grocery store?

ESPERANZA
(unconcerned)
How would I know? Maybe she had some other errand to run.

                         MARK
And not tell me?

                       ESPERANZA
I didn't know you were her scheduling secretary.

                         MARK
No. It's just…. Never mind.

                       ESPERANZA
What is it?

                         MARK
                    (anxiously)
I like to know where she is…. Just in case, you know.

                       ESPERANZA
Does she know you want to know where she is all the time?

                         MARK
We talked about it when she decided to move back home from
Texas.

                       ESPERANZA
Something must have distracted her or got in the way of
getting the groceries first.

                         MARK
She could have called to tell me her plans changed. She
knows it's important to me.

                       ESPERANZA
                 (sympathetically)
I know, sweetie.

                         MARK
Not that it would happen, but…

                       ESPERANZA
Well, Big Brother, no worries. I'm here.

                         MARK
Yeah, I know. But with you just out of the hospital and,
and…. I don't know. Aren't I supposed to be supervising
you?

ESPERANZA
Hang tight. You'll be okay. We'll supervise each other.

BLACKOUT

SCENE FIVE

> (MARK is on the sofa
> with his head in his
> hands. ESPERANZA is
> circling the room.)

MARK

I really hate this.

ESPERANZA

Hate is a pretty strong word.

MARK

Yeah, I know. It's just … never mind.

ESPERANZA

What is it? I'm not that fragile. In fact, I feel pretty
clear-headed right now.

MARK
(sarcastically)
Do you now?

ESPERANZA

Maybe it's breathing air that hasn't been recycled over and
over. That's probably it. I feel oxygenated!

MARK

Good for you, Dear Sister.

ESPERANZA

Hey! I know sarcasm when I hear it. What's really eating
you?

MARK
(looking up to her)
Why did you lie to me?

ESPERANZA

What? I didn't-

> (MARK shifts awkwardly to the chair.)

MARK

You lied to me. Caridad told me Doctor Greene would be coming by here today to see you after you got out. You said you won't see him until Thursday, the fifth. So, which is it? Is he stopping here today or not?

ESPERANZA

Big Brother, would I have spent all that time on the phone trying to get my meds straightened out if I knew Doctor Greene was coming here today? I wouldn't do that, would I? You know how frustrating it is to talk to hospitals and doctors' offices and insurance companies.

MARK

Well, I guess. I thought you were gas lighting me. But why would Caridad say you told her he would be coming here? She wouldn't be pulling something on me.

ESPERANZA

Oh, but you thought I would?

                    (ESPERANZA begins pacing behind the sofa.)

MARK

Come on, Ranza, that's not fair. Who am I supposed to trust more, the sister who takes care of me or the sister who returns to town after a vacation and almost immediately drives off the road on purpose?

ESPERANZA

You said you could see yourself doing the same thing.

MARK

Yeah, but I'm already certified. What were you doing? Trying to horn in on my territory?

ESPERANZA

Big Brother, you don't hold a monopoly on doing crazy shit. Not in this family. Our fathers beat you to that a long time ago.
                    (stopping)
Why Momma had such a hankering for fruitcake, I don't know.

MARK

Maybe I shouldn't have believed your story.

Between Panic and Desire

                              ESPERANZA
It's not a story. It's exactly what happened.

                                MARK
Don't give me that. You make stories up all the time.

                              ESPERANZA
I do not.

                                MARK
Then how do you know Caridad's dad was nutty? He was long
gone before I was born. Momma never said anything to me.
Never said anything about my father either. The only one we
ever knew anything about was your dad and that's only
because he never fooled around on Momma and lasted a lot
longer. She won't speak a word about my dad or Caridad's
after what they did.

                              ESPERANZA
Do you blame her?

                                MARK
We ain't talking about Momma. We're talking about you.

                              ESPERANZA
We'll just have to wait until Cari is back. She'll tell
you.

                    (ESPERANZA moves toward the door as MARK
                    speaks.)

                                MARK
Tell me what? That Momma had three babies by three daddies,
each man crazier than the last? She ain't never heard that
from Momma and she certainly don't know it from personal
experience. Caridad only knows her daddy refused to marry
Momma and probably fathered two kids with Aunt Shirley. And
she was too young to remember anything about my daddy
before Momma divorced him. I had to listen to Aunt Shirley
every Wednesday evening after choir practice tell Momma how
put out she was all those years cuz Momma wasn't keen on
seeing our fathers straying from home to swing with their
sisters-in-law, like they was common property for all the
Hogsdon sisters. Aunt Shirley made a point of complaining
Momma always found the best husbands for herself when she
and Aunt Janet couldn't find half as good where they was

lookin'. Didn't help none that our daddies were more than
eager to oblige them.

                    ESPERANZA
            (turning to face MARK)
What are you doing?

                    MARK
What am I doing what?

                    ESPERANZA
All of a sudden you were talking like you just walked out
of a backwoods holler or something.

                    MARK
How am I supposed to talk?

                    ESPERANZA
I don't know how you're supposed to talk. I'm just saying
you started sounding like a stereotypical hillbilly.

                    MARK
It's just one of those things.

                    ESPERANZA
Yeah, that's what Momma would say. One of those things.
Anyway, when did Cari say she'd be back?

                    MARK
That's the point. Remember?

                                        BLACKOUT

SCENE SIX

>   (ESPERANZA is sitting behind
>   the sofa facing upstage. MARK
>   is lying on the sofa. CARIDAD
>   enters from upstage.)

                    CARIDAD
What's going on with you two?

                    MARK
I'm practicing how to lie still in a pine box and Ranza is
waiting for a bus now that her driver's permit has been
confiscated.

                    ESPERANZA
It wasn't confiscated. I surrendered it voluntarily.

                    CARIDAD
Yes, that was a smart thing to do. Turning in your license
went a long way to convincing the doctors you're healthy.

                    MARK
Why is it that performing like dogs fearing a rolled-up
newspaper across the snout goes farther in establishing
sanity than asserting one's independence and resolve?

                    ESPERANZA
                    (turning around)
Are you saying that when I go along with treatment
recommendations, I'm not making an independent decision?

                    MARK
What do you think?

>   (ESPERANZA stands and moves directly behind the
>   sofa.)

                    CARIDAD
Don't play his games. Agreeing with people who are more
knowledgeable than you on a subject is not a sign of
dependence or weakness.

                    ESPERANZA
                    (leaning down to MARK's face)
You're not playing a game, Big Brother, are you?

                    MARK
Not one bit, Dear Sister.
                    (MARK sits up. ESPERANZA kneels behind him and
                    rests her chin on the sofa back near his head.)
I was merely pointing out that going along with others
typically involves a degree of submission. Submission to
the will of others is hardly a characteristic of a mature,
independent person.

                    CARIDID
Mark, you are applying an awfully broad concept to
circumstances that have many other variables at play.
Agreeing with someone is not always a sign of wimping out.

                    MARK
It seems to be every time you are home and we order pizza
and decide the toppings.

                    (CARIDAD walks to the chair and sits.)

                    CARIDAD
Accepting that I do not like sausage on pizza does not
qualify as forcing you to bend to my will. I have offered
to order a pizza with sausage on one half or ordering two
pizzas.

                    MARK
You know very well those alleged compromises leave me
looking like a glutton, since either way I end up with four
slices or a whole pie all to myself.

                    ESPERANZA
I would never think of you as gluttonous, Big Brother.

                    (ESPERANZA lies down behind the sofa.)

                    MARK
Thank you.

                    ESPERANZA
Although now that I think about it, I bet some other of the
seven cardinal sins might apply.

                    CARIDAD
Taking an inventory of someone else's character defects is
never a good use of time.

                    (MARK kneels on the sofa to look down on
                    ESPERANZA behind the sofa.)

                              MARK
Except now I'm curious what Ranza thinks I'm guilty of.
Come on, Dear Sister, what mortal sins should I be praying
to be forgiven for?

                            ESPERANZA
                    (rising back on her knees so she is face to
                    face with MARK)
Well, I would knock out pride right off the bat.

                              MARK
That has me disheartened.

                            CARIDAD
Mark, you know quite well you are never satisfied with your
accomplishments and never boast about anything.

                            ESPERANZA
                    (still looking directly into his eyes)
On the other hand, lust is probably your most outstanding
quality.

                            CARIDAD
Really? I would say anger.

                            ESPERANZA
                    (standing)
That is big. But he spends more time thinking about who he
wants than who he resents.

                              MARK
Since when did you become a mind reader?

                    (MARK lies back again on the sofa.)

                            CARIDAD
One doesn't have to be telepathic to recognize when someone
has a sexual interest in someone else. When we're out in
public, especially around the campus or on Philly Street,
your head can move three hundred sixty degrees.

                            ESPERANZA
I bet all the eye candy provided by IUP students is one of
the foremost reasons you came back to live here.

MARK
It's an added perk, but no, I live in Indiana PA due to my disabilities and not being able to earn a living after those bastards harassed me out of my job.

CARIDAD
Which means anger tops lust. What about the other deadly sins?

ESPERANZA
(straddling the sofa back and counting with her fingers)
Let's see. We did pride, gluttony, anger, and lust. There's greed, envy, and, and…. What's the other one?

CARIDAD
Sloth.

ESPERANZA
Ooh! That's a tough one.

MARK
Does that mean you are ruling out greed and envy?

ESPERANZA
Of course, Big Brother! You have never been covetous of other people's money or possessions.

CARIDAD
Look at how upset you have been about your benefits being cut prematurely due to your inheritance. That demonstrates depths of character.

MARK
Well, depths of something.

ESPERANZA
See? That's why we took pride off the table right away. You are modest to a fault, as they say, Big Brother.

CARIDAD
Ever wonder why they say that?

MARK
Not at all.

                    ESPERANZA
Too much modesty leads people to think one has low self-
esteem. Just look how bad Mark feels when he receives a
compliment. Isn't that right, Big Brother?

                      MARK
I don't feel bad. I just don't like attention placed on me
by others for any reason, whether it's criticism or praise.

                    ESPERANZA
              (standing again)
Except you don't mind when your sisters discuss your
faults.

                      MARK
I do so. Just go ahead and say I'm a lazy sonofabitch and
we're done.

                     CARIDAD
Tempting as it is to agree with you given your supine
position, I can't see sloth being one of your bad
qualities.

                    ESPERANZA
I agree, Big Sister. Our brother has proven far too
productive in his lifetime to warrant being labelled lazy.

                      MARK
          (propping his head up with one arm)
Labelled? I'm not a can of soup.

                    ESPERANZA
What would you call it?

                     CARIDAD
Identified works.

                      MARK
Botanists identify plants.

                     CARIDAD
I think they classify plants. How about branded?

                      MARK
          (flattening back down again)
That's worse than labelled. I'll stick with identified.

ESPERANZA
Now that's settled, we can begin work on removing the two
character defects you have in abundance.

MARK
Who agreed to have them removed?

ESPERANZA
(looking down into his face again)
Why would you want to keep them?

MARK
(sitting up again)
It isn't a matter of wanting or not.

CARIDAD
It probably is, but what makes you think not?

MARK
There's no sense trying to stop me from getting angry. The
medications I'm on tamp down the nastier responses, but I
don't have any control over getting upset when I'm
triggered.

ESPERANZA
I guess so.

CARIDAD
It is something you acquired. I don't recall you ever
raising your voice before you came back from Iraq.

MARK
Regardless, it's not something I can un-acquire.

ESPERANZA
Sure, but between the meds and therapy…

CARIDAD
Not to mention venting frustrations by complaining to the
appropriate people when you have a bad experience.

MARK
Okay, okay. So, I can do something about my anger. But the
only way I'm going to stop being filled with lust is when
they stop producing bodies for me to lust after.

                    ESPERANZA
You did inherit Momma's desire for every man able to stand
up straight before lying down.

                    CARIDAD
I doubt evaluating everyone you see by how much they arouse
you is genetic.

                    MARK
You're right. It's probably a learned behavior.

                    CARIDAD
And you had a master teacher.

                    ESPERANZA
I bet Momma's already run through all the men at that
senior living place.

                    MARK
She's only been there two weeks.

                    ESPERANZA
          (laughing)
Of course, these days, she'll probably forget she knew them
and seduce them over and over.

                    MARK
Ranza!

                    CARIDAD
Ever notice that 'whore' applies only to women?

                    ESPERANZA
Slut, too.

                    MARK
Why are you looking at me?

                                        BLACKOUT

Between Panic and Desire

SCENE SEVEN

>   (MARK is lying on the sofa.
>   CARIDAD is looking out the
>   'window'. ESPERANZA is
>   playing with the men's winter
>   coat hanging by the door.)

ESPERANZA

I didn't mean to upset you, Big Brother.

MARK

It's okay.

CARIDAD

I said it's a waste of time to look at other people's defects of character.

MARK

I'd hardly call having a strong libido a defect of character.

>   (MARK grabs the pencil and notepad and writes.)

CARIDAD

Decided that one was worth using in one of your novels?

MARK

Given what I write, sure.

ESPERANZA

On a related topic, Mark claims you can't possibly know that your daddy and his daddy were almost as crazy as my daddy.

CARIDAD

I only know that from inference and from what Aunt Shirley told me.

MARK

Before or after dementia hit her?

CARIDAD

Both. Even now, Aunt Shirley is never more lucid than when she talks about her brothers-in-law.

MARK

Since her two children were fathered by one of them, she
has a lot to talk about.

> (ESPERANZA moves to the 'window'. CARIDAD sits
> in the chair.)

CARIDAD

It's a wonder Aunt Janet didn't have kids with my father or
yours, too. Mark and I are lucky to have been born after
they used up so much of their energy before going home to
Momma every night.

MARK

Momma sure was famous for being able to squeeze two cups
more cider from a basket of apples than any other woman
around.

ESPERANZA
> (turning back to the others)
I always took that literally.

MARK

You just might. Anyway, I shouldn't be talking about Momma
like that.

CARIDAD

I doubt she would complain. She probably wouldn't discuss
it with her son, but she almost likes being talked about as
a sexual being. She sees that as a positive reflection on
her looks and liberal nature, not a negative expression of
her morals.

> (ESPERANZA moves to the door and fiddles with
> the coat again.)

ESPERANZA

Momma once told me that if women want to have a choice
about what is done with their bodies when it comes to
pregnancy, they have to own the choices they make about
their bodies that lead to pregnancy, too. No sense
complaining about being knocked up if you had any
consensual role in getting there.

CARIDAD

Which explains why she had no problem having me without
marrying my father or with kicking him out of our lives.

ESPERANZA
Given the timing, I'd say Mark's father coming into the
picture precipitated your father getting the boot.

MARK
All well and good, Dear Sister, but you still haven't
proven that Cari's daddy or mine was crazy like yours. The
pharmacist routinely gives me a lecture on how important it
is to take my medications as prescribed, citing the example
of my first stepfather. As though one day off the happy
pills will make me want to streak naked down Philly Street
and masturbate in front of the Jimmy Stewart statue.

ESPERANZA
For one thing, if you were to do something that nutty, you
would find something original.

MARK
Hell, even drunken IUP students find more interesting
things to do.

CARIDAD
I'm surprised you think IUP students are the least bit
interesting.

ESPERANZA
I bet it depends on how he defines 'interesting'.

MARK
For starters, interested in my advances.

ESPERANZA
See!

CARIDAD
What do you expect? We all went there. It's not a bad
education, but it's akin to doing four more years of high
school with more free time to get laid.

ESPERANZA
                (turning suddenly from playing with her coat)
Did Cari just say, 'get laid'? Where is this earthy side of
you been hiding?

                    CARIDAD
Ranza, when it comes to that aspect of human life, I choose
to generally remain silent. I don't link my self-esteem to
knowing others are in awe of my sexual activities.

                    ESPERANZA

And I do, Big Sister?

                    MARK

I think she meant me.

          (ESPERANZA moves to the sofa and indicates she
          wants to sit where MARK is. He moves over and
          she sits.)

                    ESPERANZA
You do take after Momma in that respect, Big Brother. I may
not be as jealous as Aunt Shirley or Aunt Janet about the
men you seem to find so easily, but there have been times I
wished one of them would notice my charms on the way in or
out of your life.

                    CARIDAD
Regardless, we already established that Mark has no
interest in being known for his ability to attract men or
any other quality he possesses.

                    ESPERANZA
What's left then?

                    MARK
Does it matter? The point is that I don't want to be known
period.

                    CARIDAD
That sounds odd coming from a writer. Don't you want to
build an audience?

                    MARK
That's different. I want my books and stuff to be read. But
the focus is on my work, not me.

                    ESPERANZA
Aren't they the same thing?

                    CARIDAD
I would think you'd want people to say, 'Look, a new novel
by Mark Forrester!'

                     MARK
Name recognition is okay. But there's no benefit to me the
person being the focus of attention. Being noticed can lead
to becoming a target. It's the predator who lurks in the
shadows, not the prey.

          (CARIDAD leans in closer to MARK.)

                   CARIDAD
Is that what you are, Mark, a predator?

          (ESPERANZA shifts closer to MARK.)

                  ESPERANZA
No, he's more like a flower attracting pollinators. You may
not like it, but you can't help yourself.

                   CARIDAD
Ranza's onto something there, sweetie. Being attractive to
others is effortless for you.

                  ESPERANZA
I think it's nice you don't let that go to your head, but
as you just said you do use it to fulfill your cravings.
You need to look the way you do even though you take no
special pride in it.

                     MARK
Need to look this way?

                   CARIDAD
          (leaning back into the chair)
We would never have found you wanting to drive straight
into a tree until airbags were perfected. You would fear
the impact might damage your features and ruin future
opportunities to writhe and coil with whomever you fancied
that day.

                         MARK
There are many more reasons for me not to drive off the
road into a tree than concern about my facial features.
Chief among them is I would not want to appear nuttier than
I already am, followed by I would not want the attention
such an act would draw.

                        CARIDAD
That reminds me. Did you save the papers with the articles
about the accident?

                         MARK
                    (to ESPERANZA)
You might want to start a memory book to document your
slide into the abyss. I think Cari's upset I never started
one.

        (ESPERANZA shifts away from MARK on the sofa.)

                       ESPERANZA
I'm not sliding into any abyss. That was a one-off affair.

                        CARIDAD
Why would you think I wanted you to keep memorabilia
related to your condition?

                         MARK
Don't you want records of events in our lives saved for
future review and posterity?

                       ESPERANZA
Personally, I rather like the idea of removing all traces
of my existence as they happen.

                        CARIDAD
Can you imagine the storage space required if everyone kept
track of everything the way presidents and famous writers
do?

                       ESPERANZA
For one thing, just think of the hubris involved in making
a decision to hold onto so much.

                         MARK
You don't need to hold onto stuff for posterity if you do
it right. Take one look at the Gospels and see how little
the difference would make if they had a presidential
library full of material on Jesus.

                         ESPERANZA
Maybe we ought to rethink whether Big Brother is guilty of
sinful pride if he's comparing himself to Jesus.

                         CARIDAD
I wouldn't go that far. He does act the martyr though.

                         MARK
Hey! Since when do I act like a martyr?

                         CARIDAD
Where to begin?

                         MARK
I have diagnosed physical and mental conditions that limit
my functioning here and in society. I don't make a big deal
of them. I don't whine and complain that it's not fair that
I am burdened with these problems.

                         CARIDAD
True, you are a model of behavior when it comes to not
fussing.

                         MARK
What else is there, then?

                         ESPERANZA
I think that's Cari's point, Big Brother.

                         MARK
What are you talking about?

                         ESPERANZA
It's not what you say. It's how you perceive yourself and
the world.

                         MARK
I try to perceive myself and my world honestly and
objectively. This is my reality.

                              CARIDAD
Okay, Mark, then be honest. When was the last time you
thought of yourself as being anything but disabled?

                                             BLACKOUT

SCENE EIGHT

>   (MARK is on the sofa looking
>   out. CARIDAD and ESPERANZA
>   are standing behind the sofa
>   looking at him.)

MARK

I can't believe you think I don't look at my abilities or
make use of them.

CARIDAD

Not really.

>   (MARK rises unsteadily, reaching for his cane
>   too late. He sits back down.)

MARK

Who has been cooking supper lo these many months? Who has
been writing the great American novel for the last three
years while also churning out eight romances to try to earn
money? For that matter, who has been hooking up with men
left and right ever since he got back from Afghanistan? I'm
quite active given my limits.

>   (ESPERANZA and CARIDAD gradually begin to move
>   away from the sofa but continue to face MARK.)

ESPERANZA

What happened to modesty?

MARK

If you're going to talk about my looks as you have and then
slander me for not making use of the talents God has
bestowed on me, I might as well point out that my Grindr
profile has been overwhelmingly effective.

CARIDAD

That might explain your views on current IUP students.

ESPERANZA

Actually, I was referring to the big, literary novel you've
been working on.

CARIDAD

Which, by the way, you haven't mentioned for, what was it?
Lo these many months.

                          MARK
I've run out of inspiration for the moment. That's all.

                        CARIDAD
That's been obvious.

                       ESPERANZA
You really haven't worked on any other projects recently
either.

                        CARIDAD
You just write down quips and aphorisms when they come to
you.

                       ESPERANZA
Your notepad must contain some gems that inspire you by
now.

                        CARIDAD
Nothing has taken the place of the hours you spent writing
except cooking supper.

                       ESPERANZA
We all could starve when your creative juices are flowing.
Instead, we're all gaining weight.

                          MARK
It's nothing. I hit an impasse. I needed a break. Do you
have any idea how difficult it is to stare at a partly-
completed book and not know how to bring it back on track?
That requires a good knock upside the head to start rolling
again.

                       ESPERANZA
That sounds a lot worse than just losing inspiration, Big
Brother.

                          MARK
You wouldn't understand.

                        CARIDAD
There's that double standard. When you're writing, you
can't wait to describe your experience. When you aren't
writing, you tell us we can't understand what that's like.

MARK
Because you can't. You don't know what it's like to be creatively dry.

ESPERANZA
I've got news for you. Everyone runs up against losing faith in their ability or finding the road to further success blocked.

MARK
You mean blocked by a tree you decided to slam into.

CARIDAD
Why do creative people think they're the only ones who suffer when failing to accomplish what they're inspired to accomplish?

ESPERANZA
They think it's a higher calling.

CARIDAD
Or there's more at stake with their egos.

MARK
Is this some theory you're developing on the fly or something you read online?

CARIDAD
Does it matter? If it rings true, does it need outside approval?

(DR. GREENE appears upstage. CARIDAD and ESPERANZA are nearing the edges of the room.)

MARK
It needs to have the underlying premise verified. Since when do creative people think they are the only ones who suffer when failing to accomplish what they are inspired to accomplish?

DR. GREENE
For starters, when they choose to run off the road into a tree just to have the experience and without thinking of the consequences.

MARK
What?

                    DR. GREENE
You heard me.

                    MARK
But I never did that.

                    DR. GREENE
You certainly did. Why do you think you were in the
hospital until this morning?

                    MARK
I wasn't in the hospital. Ranza was!

                    ESPERANZA
No, Mark. You were in the hospital.

                    CARIDAD
You're just experiencing short term memory loss. Dr. Greene
told you to expect this.

                    MARK
Dr. Greene? He's the new psychiatrist at Regional. I
haven't met him yet.

          (DR. GREENE now stands behind the sofa.)

                    DR. GREENE
You've been under my care for the last eleven days, Mark,
ever since the paramedics took you to Regional after the
crash.

                    MARK
That's impossible. I've been right here at home.

                    ESPERANZA
Mark, you have been denying you drove the car off the road
as often as you have been admitting it.

                    MARK
I don't remember.

                    DR. GREENE
Okay. Let me explain, Mark. You were released from the
hospital this morning. Eleven days ago, you turned off
Route 119 heading toward the towns of Desire and Panic just
north of Punxsutawney. You told a friend you were finally
going to go up there and take pictures of the signs to post

                    DR. GREENE (cont.)
on Facebook for your Army buddies. You drove your car into
a tree on the road between Desire and Panic. You told the
paramedics you did it on purpose just to have the
experience but planned it so you wouldn't get hurt. Aside
from some bruises from the airbags, you were fine. But we
had to hospitalize you because this was a psychotic
episode. You assured us you would never do anything like it
again.

                    MARK
No, no. It was Ranza. I didn't drive off the road. I don't
remember driving off the road.

                    CARIDAD
It's a normal psychological defense to block the memory of
an act someone is ashamed of.

                    MARK
How can I be ashamed of something I never did?

                    DR. GREENE
That's the point, Mark. By blocking the memory, you believe
you never did it and therefore you don't carry the guilt
for what occurred during the psychotic episode.

                    MARK
Then why did Ranza say she was the one who ran her car into
the tree?

                    ESPERANZA
That's another defense mechanism.

          (ESPERANZA backs out of the light and exits.)

                    DR. GREENE
We discussed Esperanza yesterday. Remember?

                    MARK
She's my younger sister. She was just here.

                    DR. GREENE
Nobody has been here except you and me.

                    MARK
No! Ranza's here! So is Caridad! I was just talking to
them!

                        DR. GREENE
I know.

                        CARIDAD
I'm just a part of you that takes care of things.

            (CARIDAD backs out of the light and exits.)

                        MARK
No, no, no! They're my sisters. I was just talking with
them!

                        DR. GREENE
Mark, you were talking to yourself. You don't have any
siblings.

                        MARK
I don't understand. Why would I lie about having two
sisters?

                        DR. GREENE
You aren't lying. In this moment, you believe you have two
sisters. They are manifestations of the qualities you
associate most strongly with your mother. They are your way
of coping with your mother's dementia, her inability to
take care of you any longer, her sudden absence.

                        MARK
It isn't sudden. We planned it for several months. She
wanted to go to Wilkes-Barre where her sisters already were
in a senior living facility. I knew that. I helped her.

                        DR. GREENE
Yes, of course. Understandably, that has been a traumatic
experience for you. Someone with pre-existing psychological
trauma like you have from your tours of duty can have
difficulty accepting further trauma. You responded, in
part, to your mother's departure by creating these sisters
who are going to help you. They only exist in your mind.

                        MARK
They were just here. We were talking. They were here!

DR. GREENE

I know, Mark. I was concerned when you told me yesterday
your sisters would take care of you when you got home from
the hospital. We hadn't heard from any sisters and you said
your mother was your only family when you were admitted.
That's why I told you I would stop by to see you. I have an
obligation to make sure you are safe after you have been
discharged. Now, I have a better grasp of what is
happening. I think we can start making more progress in
your treatment. We have some work to do. Do you want to
start now?

MARK

I don't know. I guess.

(DR. GREENE sits down.)

DR. GREENE

Good. We'll start with the core issue. When was the last
time you thought of yourself as being anything other than
disabled?

BLACKOUT

SCENE NINE

>（ESPERANZA is on the sofa.
> CARIDAD is standing, speaking
> on the telephone. They are
> wearing different clothes
> than before.)

CARIDAD
That's right. … I am calling about my brother … Mark
Forrester … My name? … Caridad Hogsdon … No, Hogsdon … No,
we have different surnames because he's my half-brother. …
Why does this matter? I could be Indira Gandhi for all you
know. … No, Indira Gandhi is not a singer. She was the
prime minister of India and I was making a little joke and
I really don't need to be explaining this—what? … Really? …
Two hours ago? … Do you know who picked him up? … Okay,
thanks.

(CARIDAD hangs up the telephone.)

ESPERANZA
What happened?

CARIDAD
They say he was picked up this morning by his mother.

ESPERANZA
Should we check whether Momma is still where she's supposed
to be?

CARIDAD
What do you think?

ESPERANZA
Seems kinda farfetched.

CARIDAD
I know. But what in this family isn't?

ESPERANZA
Do you think Mark's playing a game?

CARIDAD
That's the likeliest scenario. Although…

ESPERANZA
What?

CARIDAD
Did Mark know when you were coming back from vacation?

ESPERANZA
I don't think so.

CARIDAD
But he knew you were going away.

ESPERANZA
Of course.

CARIDAD
And I told him I would be in sometime this week depending
on the weather.

ESPERANZA
When was that?

CARIDAD
We talked the day before the accident.

ESPERANZA
The day I left on vacation.

CARIDAD
I just wonder…

    (CARIDAD pulls out her cell phone and places a
    call.)

ESPERANZA
Who are you calling?

CARIDAD
Augie.

ESPERANZA
Oh, I see. Mother as in Mother Hen.

                    CARIDAD
No answer…. I think Augie only has a landline like Mark.
                (CARIDAD hangs up and puts the phone away.)
I bet Mother picked up Mark from the hospital this morning.
Knowing them, they went to Home for breakfast or went to
get pie at that place down near the power plant.

                    ESPERANZA
Sounds plausible. But why didn't you pick him up?

                    CARIDAD
The nurse on duty yesterday told me Mark didn't have any
sisters, so I couldn't visit him or get any information.
The psych unit is pretty careful about access and this
nurse didn't seem too interested in explanations. I told
her that Mark always jokes he's an only child.

                (CARIDAD sits on the sofa and picks up the
                cards on the table. She plays solitaire while
                ESPERANZA wanders around the room examining
                little things.)

                    ESPERANZA
He is, after a fashion. Near as I know, his daddy didn't
have any other kids. Otherwise Mark wouldn't be inheriting
the entire estate.

                    CARIDAD
I rather doubt my father will be leaving me much more than
a twentieth of next to nothing.

                    ESPERANZA
Twentieth?

                    CARIDAD
It could be. Pop is a breeder, pure and simple. He didn't
contest that Aunt Shirley's two boys were his. By last
count, Pop had ten more children by four other mothers.
That was twelve years ago or so.

                    ESPERANZA
Do you know if he's still alive?

                    CARIDAD
To the extent that the Internet is up-to-date with
obituaries and he didn't die on some street with no
identification.

ESPERANZA
That's a morbid way of thinking.

CARIDAD
Speaking of which, do we know how Mark found out about his father's death.

ESPERANZA
Letter from a lawyer assigned to handle the estate. It arrived the same day we took Momma to Wilkes-Barre.

CARIDAD
He didn't mention it to me.

ESPERANZA
How'd you find out then?

CARIDAD
From Momma. All she said was Mark's dad passed and Mark was inheriting over a million dollars.

ESPERANZA
She told me she was glad that Mark would have money to take care of him and wouldn't be dependent on his disability benefits and all.

CARIDAD
I guess. Maybe it will curb his enthusiasm for complaining to companies about mistakes they make.

ESPERANZA
You think?

CARIDAD
Getting coupons and rebates for stuff from those companies is probably his second biggest source of income.

ESPERANZA
It can't be more than the royalties from his novels.

CARIDAD
I don't know. He always pooh-poohs the income generated by his writing. And he really is obsessed about correcting corporate errors.

ESPERANZA
At least it's a harmless obsession, unlike…

CARIDAD

Well, apparently the doctor at Regional thinks he won't be harmful or they wouldn't be discharging him.

ESPERANZA

Unlike my daddy.

CARIDAD

Oh, yes. That's very sad. Do you visit him?

ESPERANZA

Every Father's Day. But to him, I'm just some nice girl he just met. After I leave, he doesn't have a daughter.

CARIDAD

That's a shame.

ESPERANZA

I don't know. He's comfortable and otherwise healthy. I can almost get to the point where I envy him. He has no cares or concerns. He just exists, every day astonishingly new.

CARIDAD

Makes you wonder, doesn't it? We can have a lifetime of experiences and when our brains decide to stop remembering we're suddenly in a new reality, as though the whole world has changed.

ESPERANZA

The whole world does from that one perspective.

CARIDAD

It's the only perspective we have.

ESPERANZA

He still has episodes when some awful experience sweeps through his mind and triggers him to do the things that got him institutionalized. He's never violent, just, just…. What's the word? … Ecstatic.

CARIDAD

Your father certainly provided fodder for stories. Whenever friends would start offering embarrassing parent moments, I would trump them all by saying my stepfather—well, one of my stepfathers—tore off his clothes, ran through town, and started masturbating in front of the Jimmy Stewart statue.

ESPERANZA
I would tell that story, too, except it's my own father.

(CARIDAD stops playing cards and settles back
in the sofa. ESPERANZA sits in the chair.)

CARIDAD
You know, nowadays, people don't know who Jimmy Stewart is
or don't get why Indiana Pennsylvania has a statue honoring
him.

ESPERANZA
I've always had enough trouble convincing people that
Indiana is a small city in PA as well as a Midwestern
state.

CARIDAD
I tell them it's just like having Washington the city and
Washington the state.

ESPERANZA
I gave up. Now, I just tell people I grew up outside of
Pittsburgh, like Pittsburgh is some big building.

CARIDAD
Are you kidding? In Texas, they don't even know where
Pittsburgh is unless they moved there from PA or Ohio. They
don't distinguish one state from another if it's above the
Mason-Dixon Line.

ESPERANZA
Are you glad you're moving back?

CARIDAD
Not for the reasons I'm moving back, but yeah. I miss
spring and fall. I even miss winter somewhat.

ESPERANZA
Speaking of which, did Phil see his shadow this morning?

CARIDAD
I don't know. I promised Mark I would watch the show with
him.

ESPERANZA
It's a little bit late for that.

                    CARIDAD
No, he told me he recorded it.

                    ESPERANZA
How could he if he's been hospitalized for eleven days?

                    CARIDAD
Knowing our brother, he sets shows up to record a month in
advance.

                    ESPERANZA
I'd forgotten about that obsession.
          (lifting the notepad from the table)
I see he still writes notes to himself about phrases he
wants to use in his writing.
          (laughing)
This one's good-smacked in the face by a satin fish.

                    CARIDAD
I guess if he had a character who wears silk gloves that
would work.

                    ESPERANZA
          (placing the notepad exactly where it was)
I can see it now. Incensed, Gloria walked up to Dustin and
struck his cheek. Whack!
          (She smacks the chair with her open palm.)
He felt as though he had been smacked in the face by a
satin fish.

                    CARIDAD
Aside from the fact he's certifiable, why does our gay
brother write over-the-top romance novels for straight
women?

                    ESPERANZA
          (waving her arm wildly)
I know! I know! Gay romance novels are all written by
middle-aged women in Iowa or Alberta or some other mind-
sucking monoculture.

                    CARIDAD
Really?

                    ESPERANZA
They get a thrill out of having a secret identity as
purveyors of homosexual man lust.

                    CARIDAD
Where on earth did you get that idea?

                    ESPERANZA
It was on The View or something. They had a bunch of women
on with their faces blurred so members of their churches
wouldn't recognize them. They all said how empowering and
invigorating it was to describe male-male romances.

                    CARIDAD
But they don't write lesbian romances?

                    ESPERANZA
Are you kidding? Everyone knows lesbians only read bad
poetry and how-to manuals.

                    CARIDAD
That's not funny.

                    ESPERANZA
Sorry.

                    CARIDAD
You're forgiven. Anyway, none of that explains why Mark
writes trashy novels for women.

          (MARK enters from the back.)

                    MARK
They aren't trash. If they were, I would sell more copies.
And I write them because I understand what excites a woman
about a man.

          (ESPERANZA jumps up and hugs MARK.)

                    ESPERANZA
Where have you been? We've been waiting and waiting.

                    MARK
What are you talking about? I've been around all morning.

                                        BLACKOUT

SCENE TEN

>(MARK and CARIDAD are
>sitting. ESPERANZA is still
>standing.)

MARK
After Doctor Greene left, I went for a walk.

CARIDAD
Who's Doctor Greene?

ESPERANZA
The new psychiatrist at Regional.

CARIDAD
The doctor made a house call?

MARK
Yep.

CARIDAD
But you were just released from the hospital this morning.

MARK
Well…

CARIDAD
Does this have anything to do with the staff at the
hospital claiming you have no sisters?

MARK
When did they do that?

CARIDAD
Yesterday, after lunch. I stopped by to see if you made any
arrangements for your discharge. The nurse refused to let
me see you.

ESPERANZA
What have you been up to, Mark?

MARK
Nothing.

ESPERANZA
Come on. You can tell us!

                    MARK
You won't like it.

                    CARIDAD
Mark, have we ever judged you?

                    MARK
Are you kidding me? When have you not? You always did moral
check-ups on me every Sunday after church to make sure I
wasn't destined to burn in hell. Well, every Sunday until
the meteor.

                    ESPERANZA
Good grief! Those were just games!

                    CARIDAD
I had forgotten about the meteor.

                    MARK
Analyzing your insane brother's shortcomings isn't a game.

                    CARIDAD
You aren't insane now and you definitely were not insane
back then.

                    ESPERANZA
Besides, we don't believe in hell anymore.

                    MARK
I do.

                    ESPERANZA
You do not.

                    MARK
Addiction recovery means the Gates of Hell have been
opened.

                    CARIDAD
Not going to write that one down on your notepad?

                    MARK
No, it's not original enough. Every AA and NA member knows
that saying.

                         ESPERANZA
Hey! Isn't doing a personal inventory using the seven
cardinal sins one of the steps?

                          MARK
You don't have to use the seven deadlies, but it's
recommended as a starting point. And yes, I had a good head
start thanks to you two trying to get me routed to
purgatory at the least.

                         CARIDAD
Mark, you know I think doing an inventory of someone else
is a waste of time.

                          MARK
Oh, right, Miss Caridad Venezia Hogsdon who looks down on
the world from above does not judge others. Please.

                         ESPERANZA
He might have you there, Cari.

                         CARIDAD
I am not having this discussion. It's just another way of
analyzing me.

                          MARK
But it's okay to analyze me?

                         CARIDAD
I didn't drive a vehicle into a tree eleven days ago. I
didn't tell people I did it just to have the experience. I
wasn't just discharged from a psych unit this morning.

                          MARK
But since I have, it's fair to pick on me?

                         CARIDAD
We aren't picking on you. We just want to know why you told
the hospital you didn't have any sisters.

                         ESPERANZA
Yeah, I don't want to be a figment of your imagination.

                         CARIDAD
Did you deny you have family again?

                    ESPERANZA
Don't you think figment is a weird word?

                    MARK
I didn't deny anything.

                    ESPERANZA
Do you think they make fig-flavored mints?

                    CARIDAD
Then why would the nurse refuse to let me see you?

                    ESPERANZA
I'm not even sure I could identify fig flavor.

                    MARK
I just didn't respond to the part about family other than
to say Momma is in a senior living facility in Wilkes-Barre
with her sisters.

                    ESPERANZA
And are fig leaves really big enough to cover an adult's
genitals?

                    MARK and CARIDAD
              (looking up at ESPERANZA)
What?

                    ESPERANZA
Never mind. I bet Mark was just too dazed by the crash and
all the attention to think clearly.

              (MARK stands and approaches the 'window'.)

                    MARK
That and they ask a lot of questions all at once when
you're admitted to a hospital. It gets confusing.

                    CARIDAD
Nice save. Wouldn't they have looked into it? After all,
why would they release you to go home if there was no one
at home to care for you?

              (MARK continues to look out rather than back at
              his sisters.)

MARK
That's easy enough. I told them my sisters were coming in
to stay and look after me until we decided what would be
the best living arrangement.

ESPERANZA
Then why was Caridad told you don't have any sisters?

MARK
I don't know. Probably the nurse you spoke with didn't know
what my discharge plans were. That wasn't settled until the
evening shift last night.

CARIDAD
And you got Augie to agree to pick you up?

MARK
How'd you know that?

CARIDAD
The hospital told me you were picked up by your mother.

ESPERANZA
Which we knew was farfetched.

MARK
Meaning you thought it was possible.

CARIDAD
That still leaves the question of your doctor-

MARK
Doctor Greene.

CARIDAD
Doctor Greene making a house call.

(MARK moves near the door.)

MARK
That one's actually kind of funny. He saw I was being
discharged to the care of my sisters and thought I was
making you two up just to go home.

ESPERANZA
By any chance is Doctor Greene good-looking?

                    MARK
Yep.

                    CARIDAD
Did you tell him you didn't have any sisters just so he
would come to the house to see if you are delusional?

                    MARK
I never said I don't have any sisters to Doctor Greene or
anyone else. They just assumed that.

                    CARIDAD
That's my point. Why would they assume that?

                    MARK
I told you, other than giving them Momma's contact
information to allow her to call and find out what was
going on with me, I didn't say nothing about my family.

                    CARIDAD
Anything.

                    MARK
What?

                    CARIDAD
You didn't say anything about your family. You said
nothing.

                    MARK
          (confused)
Yes, I said nothing. Or wait. No, I didn't say anything. …
I don't know.

                    CARIDAD
Either way, you gave Doctor Greene the impression you were
going home to two sisters he had no knowledge of from what
you had said previously.

                    ESPERANZA
Or didn't say.

                    MARK
The omission was not intentional.

                    CARIDAD
Did he tell you he was going to make a house call?

                    MARK
He might have. I'm having short term memory issues, which
he said are normal.

                    CARIDAD
Good thing you remember that.

                    MARK
Remember what?

                    CARIDAD
Don't be a smartass.

                    ESPERANZA
Anyway, he came. He saw you. What happened?

                    MARK
It was confusing. He told me I didn't have any sisters. He
said I was rationalizing why I could be home even though
Momma is gone. That freaked me out. We started talking
about my perceptions, how I knew if something was real. It
took me a few minutes to figure out how to explain it
really was just miscommunication without sounding crazy.

                    ESPERANZA
Er.

                    MARK
Thanks. Crazier.

                    CARIDAD
I take it he believed you when you explained you really
have two sisters.

                    MARK
Not at first. Uh, when he came in, I guess I was talking to
you two.

                    ESPERANZA
That's scary.

                    MARK
I know. He said we'll have to work out whether I was just
mindlessly talking out loud, dreaming, or hallucinating.

                    CARIDAD
I can see why that just reinforced in his mind that you
don't have any sisters.

                    MARK
Yep. I finally had to show him pictures and email messages.

                    CARIDAD
And that satisfied him?

                    MARK
Not completely. So, I told him to come back after lunch and
he could see for himself.

                    CARIDAD
He's coming back? Just how good looking is he?

                    MARK
You'll see.

                    ESPERANZA
You dog!

                                        BLACKOUT

SCENE ELEVEN

>   (Doctor Greene is
>   sitting on the sofa
>   talking on the phone and
>   playing with the
>   notepad.)

                    DR. GREENE
Right. … No. … No, no, that won't work. … I don't think
I'll be much longer. … It was just an odd miscommunication,
so I had to come back here. … Who? … The next time she
calls tell her that her son has been discharged and is at
home with her two daughters. … I don't care if you can't
find the HIPAA form. The patient said he filled one out. …
What would you want if it was your memory-impaired mother
calling about you? … Right. … No. … Right. … Okay.

>   (DR. GREENE hangs up the telephone. He looks
>   more closely at the notepad, intrigued. MARK
>   enters from the rear.)

                    MARK
All done, doctor?

                    DR. GREENE
Yep. Thanks for the use of your phone. I'm always
forgetting to charge my cell phone. Not a good thing for
someone on call all the time.

                    MARK
I've never bothered with a cell phone. Not worth adding to
my budget. Besides, I already have enough voices in my
head. No need to add to them.

                    DR. GREENE
Voices? You denied hearing voices.

                    MARK
I'm joking. Sorry.

                    DR. GREENE
No worries. You know, one of the nice things about texting
is you can use emojis to clarify intent. Sometimes they're
better signals than live facial expressions. My mother uses
them a lot. I think she's more adept using her smartphone
than I am.

                    MARK
Which one of you has more time to play with it?

                    DR. GREENE
True enough.

          (MARK sits in the chair.)

                    MARK
Speaking of mothers, I wasn't eavesdropping or anything,
but did I hear you say something about someone's mother to
the person on the phone?

                    DR. GREENE
Oh, yes. Your mother called the hospital. I guess you
haven't had a chance to tell her you've been discharged. I
told them that if she calls back to let her know.

                    MARK
Yep. She'll be worried. At least until she forgets she
called.

                    DR. GREENE
Maybe you should call her now.

                    MARK
First, I have to get over finding out that she called
Social Security to tell them I'm a millionaire and don't
need to receive benefits any longer.

                    DR. GREENE
You know she didn't do it maliciously. She was happy for
you.

                    MARK
I suppose. It's still a mess I have to deal with.

                    DR. GREENE
Mark, you allow the frustrations of handling problems with
people you see as incompetent to control you. My suggestion
is to stop trying to fix problems when you start feeling
triggered. Do something else. Cook. Take a walk.

                    MARK
I'd just as soon not have the problems.

DR. GREENE
We all would. At least your half-sisters are here to help
you take care of some of the problems.

MARK
Um, doctor, I'd appreciate it if you wouldn't refer to them
as half-sisters. Makes them sound like they're cut in half
or rank below full sisters.

DR. GREENE
Of course. I apologize.

MARK
Oh, no worries.

DR. GREENE
Does your mother know your sisters are helping you out?

MARK
Cari called Momma to talk about moving up here from Texas.
But she had planned that move as soon as we started looking
for a facility for Momma. She wanted to be able to visit
her more often and was kinda over living in Texas.

DR. GREENE
Fortuitously, she can help you, too.

MARK
Of course. She never said she was moving here to keep an
eye on me. Everything was managed pretty well. But I get
the impression she was concerned about me living alone.

DR. GREENE
I can't say for certain that concern was justified before
the accident.

MARK
And now you think it's good I'll have some supervision?

DR. GREENE
Now that I know your sisters are real, yes.

MARK
You know that was a one-off thing.

                    DR. GREENE
I accept your rationale and your commitment not to do
something like that again. I wouldn't have agreed to you
being discharged otherwise.

                       MARK
But there's the matter now of the hallucinations and
dreams. Those threw me for a loop.

                    DR. GREENE
As they should. You had the perfect storm of coming home to
finding out your disability benefits had been stopped by
your mother, her recent move to a memory care unit, your
guilt about the accident, your concerns about how your
sisters were going to deal with the accident, your father's
death, and the news about your inheritance. That's a lot to
put on the shoulders of someone who already suffers from
PTSD and depression, is four or five years into addiction
recovery, and has writer's block.

                       MARK
Are you telling me writer's block is a psychological
disorder?

                    DR. GREENE
What do you think?

           (MARK reaches for the notepad and pencil.)

                                        BLACKOUT

SCENE TWELVE

>   (MARK is on the sofa. DR.
>   GREENE is looking out the
>   'window'.)

                         DR. GREENE
I know I'm going to be opening a can of worms by asking,
but the hospital told me you were picked up this morning by
your mother. My understanding is she is in Wilkes-Barre. Is
that another example of your mind providing a different
reality than what actually happened?

                         MARK
>   (laughing)
No, doc. There's this Canadian guy, Augie, in his sixties,
who taught English at IUP before he retired. He lives down
in Johnstown. Augie used to shepherd younger gay guys to
the bars in Pittsburgh. We started calling him Mother
because he was like a Mother Hen to us.

                         DR. GREENE
And he picked you up this morning?

                         MARK
Yep.

                         DR. GREENE
>   (walking around the room)
Wow! This is one for the books. Non-existent sisters and
real sisters, two mothers, one of each sex, one real and
the other just a nickname. What else?

                         MARK
Doctor, why do you keep calling some people real and others
not? They're real to me.

                         DR. GREENE
Because objectively some are the thing defined and some are
not.

                         MARK
Doesn't that presuppose we agree on what the categories we
use objectively mean? What makes you more real than my
hallucinations and dreams this morning?

                    DR. GREENE
For starters, I have a material being

          (MARK stands and makes his way to DR. GREENE.)

                    MARK
So did the sisters I saw this morning. At least I thought
they did.

                    DR. GREENE
Our perceptions sometimes deceive us into believing
something that additional information proves is not real.

                    MARK
          (MARK reaches out to touch DR. GREENE's arm.)
But additional information can confirm the conclusion, too.

                    DR. GREENE
          (awkwardly, as MARK grasps his arm)
Well, of course.

          (CARIDAD and ESPERANZA enter from the rear.
          MARK releases DR. GREENE's arm and steps back)

                    CARIDAD
Doctor, are you still here?

                    DR. GREENE
We were just about to find out, I think.

                    MARK
Cari, how do you know something is real?

                    CARIDAD
As opposed to fake?

                    MARK
No, smartass. As opposed to illusion.

                    CARIDAD
I don't ever really think about it.

                    DR. GREENE
That's the answer you are going to get from ninety-nine
percent of the people you ask. People generally do not
question existence.

ESPERANZA
Why would they? Like I've told you, nothing outside my ken
is real. If I can't see it, smell it, smack it, or suck it,
it isn't there, doesn't exist. And never trust anything you
hear. You never know if those are actual people talking or
voices in your head or just an air conditioner.

MARK
A what?

ESPERANZA
An air conditioner, silly. Haven't you ever noticed that a
room air conditioner heard from another room sounds like
people talking.

MARK
That must be one of those things.

DR. GREENE
Things?

CARIDAD
Members of our family are not just certifiable, doctor. We
all have our peculiar ideas of what is odd or notable.
Momma always said they were one of those things.

ESPERANZA
Speaking of certifiable, doctor, you ought to look up my
Pop's medical records. They're a hoot!

MARK
If you do, just remember I am not related to him by blood.

DR. GREENE
I'm glad this family is so comfortable with psychological
conditions.

ESPERANZA
We kind of have to. Mark once had an idea for an app that
would report the mental conditions of everyone in our
twisted family tree so we would know whether to visit or
stay away.

MARK
No, I didn't.

                    ESPERANZA
Somebody did.

                    CARIDAD
Sounds more like something Momma would come up with.

                    MARK
I don't even have a cell phone.

                    ESPERANZA
I don't blame you. Cell phones are the number one source of
voices in your head.

                    MARK
I don't have voices in my head either.

                    CARIDAD
No need to get defensive, Mark.

                    ESPERANZA
Yeah. You don't want to add paranoia to the list of things
you have. Right, doc?

                    MARK
Definitely not after he just told me I can include writer's
block in the list.

                    ESPERANZA
Really? Congratulations on your new disorder!

                    DR. GREENE
That reminds me. Mark, you wrote on this pad about spring
being in a quantum state of having six more weeks or not
until you know whether Phil sees his shadow. That's a very
perceptive observation.

                    MARK
Hey, we never watched the ceremony!

                    BLACKOUT

SCENE THIRTEEN

                              (MARK is on the sofa using a
                              TV remote. He sets the remote
                              down.)

                    MARK (V.O.)
It's odd. They declare me crazy, but a few miles north
folks make such a big fuss about a rodent forecasting the
weather, an animal they'd shoot on sight if it was
rummaging in their vegetable gardens. … I guess when a lot
of people agree to believe something, it makes it real.
                    (looking at the empty chair)
Cari, did you take that psych class at IUP where they
talked about perception and reality? … Yep. … I thought the
people out there might be interested.
                    (MARK nods toward the audience.)
I told you about the people out there. … Oh, that's right.
I told Ranza. … Okay. Here's an example. I place a two-
dollar bill on the table and leave.
                    (MARK places a bill on the table.)
Ranza, you come in. The two-dollar bill catches your
attention as you pass through the room.
                    (glancing up behind the sofa as if someone is
                    standing there)
Right. That's why it needs to be a two-dollar bill. Anyway,
Cari comes in later and takes the money.
                    (MARK removes the bill from the table.)
Well, you are the hardened criminal in the family, aren't
you? Now, Ranza comes back. She sees the money is gone. She
places another two-dollar bill on the table.
                    (MARK places a new bill on the table.)
Mind you, she doesn't know Cari took the first one. She
doesn't know what happened to it at all.
                    (MARK straightens himself up and cocks his
                    head)
I come home. I see the two-dollar bill is still there. In
my mind, the two-dollar bill was always on the table. In
Ranza's mind, there are two two-dollar bills, the one she
saw initially and the one she placed on the table. And when
Cari comes home, she can't understand how the two-dollar
bill can still be there. In her mind, it's been in her
wallet. So, she looks in her wallet—
                    (MARK produces the other bill.)
and finds the original two-dollar bill. She has no idea
where the second two-dollar bill came from or how someone
knew to put it in the exact same spot. … Yep. No one has

                         MARK (V.O.) (cont.)
all the information to definitively say what happened. We
each have our own perception of reality. Ranza is right.
Reality is only that which is currently within my ken. And
I ought never to trust what I hear.

                (The telephone rings. MARK answers it.)

                              MARK
Hello … Oh, hello, Doctor Greene. Thanks for returning my
call. … Yep. … Great.
                (MARK picks up the notepad and pen.)
Okay … February fifth … ten o'clock. … Yep. … I'm sure
Mother can drive me. … Thanks, doc. … I look forward to
finally meeting you. Welcome to Indiana PA!

                                        BLACKOUT

                         END